P9-AEY-668

Dear Toni

Cyndi Sand-Eveland

Tundra Books

First paperback edition published by Tundra Books, 2010
Text and interior art copyright © 2008 by Cyndi Sand-Eveland

Published in Canada by Tundra Books,
75 Sherbourne Street, Toronto, Ontario M5A 2P9

Published in the United States by Tundra Books of Northern New York,
P.O. Box 1030, Plattsburgh, New York 12901

Library of Congress Control Number: 2007943134

All rights reserved. The use of any part of this publication
reproduced, transmitted in any form or by any means, electronic,
mechanical, photocopying, recording, or otherwise, or stored
in a retrieval system, without the prior written consent of
the publisher – or, in case of photocopying or other reprographic
copying, a licence from the Canadian Copyright Licensing Agency –
is an infringement of the copyright law.

Library and Archives Canada Cataloguing in Publication

Sand-Eveland, Cyndi
    Dear Toni / Cyndi Sand-Eveland.

ISBN 978-1-77049-249-3

    I. Title.

PS8637.A539D42 2010   jC813'.6   C2010-904434-7

We acknowledge the financial support of the Government of Canada
through the Book Publishing Industry Development Program (BPIDP)
and that of the Government of Ontario through the Ontario Media
Development Corporation's Ontario Book Initiative. We further
acknowledge the support of the Canada Council for the Arts
and the Ontario Arts Council for our publishing program.

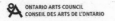
ONTARIO ARTS COUNCIL
CONSEIL DES ARTS DE L'ONTARIO

Design: Jennifer Lum
Jacket Art: Gillian Newland

Printed and bound in Canada

1 2 3 4 5 6   15 14 13 12 11 10

For

Patches, who loves a hug,

Kurt, who loves to look at faces, and

my parents, who could build and fix almost anything.

Acknowledgments

First, I want to acknowledge the BC Festival of the Arts;
I was fortunate enough to participate in the final year
of that program. Although the premise for this story
did not begin there, the inspiration and encourage-
ment to continue writing did. Many thanks to Andrea
Spalding and Ann Featherstone.

Anne Degrace, Verna Relkoff, Danielle McArthur, Fiona
Bayrock, Claudia Jane Hall, Val Speed, Robyn Sheppard,
and Haylee Eveland – who was twelve at the time – all
edited at least one draft of this story. Thank you. Also
to Liz Tanner, Diane Goldsmith, and Ann McDonnell,
who each read earlier versions and answered my
questions about teaching, many thanks.

To Eileen Deforge and her Grade-4 class at Strathcona
Elementary in Vancouver, BC, thank you for your
careful listening and insights.

Thank you also to the staff and students at Blewett and
South Nelson Elementary Schools, and to the past and
present members of my writing group.

Writing a story is one thing, but getting it into print another. Being a writer with a nasty habit of sending a manuscript out once and then filing it, I was destined to never find my way into print. Friends like Anne DeGrace and a book agent like Morty Mint are priceless to someone like me. More than you know, Morty and Anne, thank you!

It has been a wonderful journey with the people at Tundra Books, and I am immensely grateful to Kathy Lowinger, Kathryn Cole, and all the people who worked on this book. Thanks also to Gillian Newland for your work on the cover.

Last but not least, I want to thank my husband, Todd, my kids, Kohe and Mclain, and my extended family and friends. They, more than anyone, have managed to smile and nod through many a version of many a story.

I'll end with Mclain's thoughts just after the news of a book contract arrived: "Well, Mom, it looks like all your hard work and neglect of your kids has finally paid off."

Sept. 9th

HELP!!!!!!!!!!!!!!!!!!!!!!!!!!!!

Dear Whoever You Are,
    Help me! I'm being beaten and tortured and tied to a post in a burning fire. Please! Someone, please help me! SAVE ME from certain death!!!!!
    According to Mr. Mackenzie, my teacher, kids' journals are a dying art form. Well, good thing, I say! Honestly though, I'm not dying, but I am being forced to write for a hundred days. One hundred days of torture and pain. One hundred days of writing about the most boring life on the planet . . . MINE! One hundred days of writing to someone I don't even know and probably never will. One hundred days of staring at a blank page, one hundred days of the thing I hate most! ONE HUNDRED DAYS OF WRITING!
    Mr. Mackenzie has promised that he won't make us do any corrections because he's not going to read our journals. Yeah, right. He's just saying that now. Teachers always make you do corrections.
    I don't even know who you are, and the truth is, you're not even born yet. You won't be born for

another twenty-nine years! Then it'll be another eleven years before you're in 6th Grade. Who knows if there will still even be such a thing as 6th Grade? And I haven't ever been to a museum. And get the part about the museum person putting our journals in a vault for forty years, and then giving them to another 6th-Grade class to read. Who would want a journal from someone in Grade 6?

That's the other thing I hate. I hate the way adults can make kids do things they don't want to do. Like writing a journal to some kid who isn't even real! And it's unfair that we have to write on five weekends so that we get a full hundred days. I never do schoolwork on the weekends! Well – not unless I'm forced to.

We're supposed to start by explaining "The Project" that our class has to do for YOU. And I need to quit because my fingers are cramping, and they feel like they're going to fall off.

cramping fingers

blisters forming

Tortured in 6th
Grade,
Gene

Sept. 12th

<u>How I Got My Name</u>

Dear Nobody,

 Mr. Mackenzie is making us write about our names, sorry. It's called a prompt. A prompt is supposed to make it easier to get writing. He tells us what the prompt for the journal entry is, and then we have to write about that. I thought a journal was like a diary where I would get to write about *my* thoughts and how *my* life is going, not about Mr. Mackenzie's ideas. Oh well, here goes.

Dear Nobody,

 My name's Gene Tucks. I got it from my mom and dad.

Yours very untruly,
Gene

Well, I'm back. Mr. Mackenzie says that I need to spend
more than fifteen seconds on my journal entry. Maybe
I'll just write *nothing, nothing, nothing, nothing,*
nothing, nothing, nothing, nothing, nothing, nothing,
nothing, nothing, nothing, nothing, nothing, nothing,
nothing, nothing, nothing, nothing, nothing, nothing,
nothing, nothing, nothing, nothing, nothing, nothing,
nothing, nothing, nothing, nothing, nothing, nothing,
nothing, nothing, nothing, nothing, nothing, nothing,
nothing, nothing, nothing, nothing, nothing, nothing,
nothing, nothing, nothing, nothing, nothing, nothing,
nothing, nothing, nothing, nothing, nothing, nothing,
for the whole journal-writing time. I hate this and I
hate having to write about my name and I hate that
I have to write when I hate writing.

Nothingly yours,
Gene Tucks

PS
Mr. Mackenzie just looked up at me from his desk and
smiled. He thinks I just wrote a whole page. Fooled
him! The truth is I'm a nobody. Hey, in a weird sort
of way we have something in common! We're both
nobodies. But I guess we're stuck with each other.
Sorry I won't be able to read about your life. I'll bet it's

a whole lot more interesting than mine. You probably get to go to Mars for summer holidays. Am I right?

PPS
My mom and dad spelled my name G E N E, even though I was a girl, because Mom wanted to name me after her favorite uncle. I never met him because he died about a month before I was born.

I wonder who you are named after. Well, seeing as you can't even answer me, I guess I'll just keep calling you Nobody. You know, especially because you have *no body*. Get it?

From the boring life of
Gene Tucks
Only ninety-eight more days to go. I can't wait!

Sept. 13th

Background Information

Dear Somebody,
Okay, how about I call you Somebody, because if you are reading this journal forty years from now, I guess you will have a body.

Today's prompt is to tell about our lives. (Ohhhhhh, I can feel myself falling asleep all ready.)

I can't remember much of the diaper stage. Most of the stories that my parents tell are very embarrassing and I don't want to tell them to you. Mr. Mackenzie suggested that I might just want to start at 6th Grade. So here goes!

I'm brand-new to Grade 6 and to Harry Gray Elementary. I hope 6th Grade goes better than 5th.

I used to be from Pelican Lake. No one here has even heard of Pelican Lake, so we usually just tell people we're from Up North. Probably by the time you read this there won't even be a Pelican Lake. My dad says there will always be a Pelican Lake, unless it dries up, but it'll be a lake and a ghost town in a couple of years, if the mill doesn't reopen. Anyway, I guess it doesn't matter because we're not moving back. We just keep moving around, looking for a steady job for my dad. He went back to school to get his mechanic's ticket, and we're all hoping that he'll find a great job and we'll be rich! Right now, he has a part-time job in a gas station, but if it doesn't work out, we might move again. I could be in a new school before I even finish this project. That would be the only good thing about moving. Because I hate it when we move, and I need to start all over.

Last year we moved three times, so I know all about first days in new schools. My mom says first impressions are really important in school and, if I can get through the first day without getting into trouble, I can start off on the right foot. Why does everybody always say *right* is right? I mean, why doesn't she say I could start out on the *left* foot? After all, I'm left-handed. Mom doesn't really like these conversations much, and usually makes me promise not to have one with my new teacher. At least not until she or he has had a few days (I know that Mom is wishing for weeks) to see my good side more than once.

You are the first kid in the class that I'm getting to know . . . well, kind of anyway. At least you are getting to know me!

Bye for now,
Gene

PS
I wonder if you will go to my school in forty years. Maybe you'll even be in this room and at my desk. Under the edge of the top I've carved my initials, G.T., with the pointy end of my compass. If you end up in this school, be sure to look under all the desktops and try to find mine. Or, maybe my school will be part of a

museum and you and your class will get to take a trip to see an old-fashioned class. How weird is that?

Sept. 14th

Our Talents

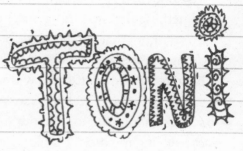

Dear Toni (I hope you don't mind me calling you Toni),

I decided calling you "Nobody" or "Somebody" really wasn't all that polite, so I came up with the name Toni. My mom has an old baby book that she bought before my brother was born. There was a list of names in there that both girls and boys could have. I kind of liked Toni and I don't know anyone else with that name. So that's the name I picked for you.

We are supposed to tell you about our talents for today's prompt. I don't really have anything to brag about. But Mr. Mackenzie says go ahead and brag — no one will ever know. I guess that's true because by the time you read this, I'll be really old. You're probably the age that I am right now. Cool!

I'm an average kid, not the smartest in the class and not the dumbest. Mr. Mackenzie says that there aren't any dumb kids, just kids with different talents. In that case, I would say that I'm a kid with a talent for doodling. Sometimes your talents help you out in school and sometimes they don't. Doodling is something that just sort of happens whenever I pick up anything that can be used for drawing or writing or doing schoolwork in general. I don't know how it will be in forty years, but the way things are now, it's not exactly what your teacher wants to find on your schoolwork or the top of your desk. I've tried convincing my mom that I could be the next Leonardo (he's a famous doodler who lived in the 1400s), but she never goes for it.

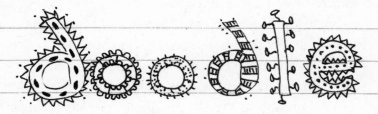

So, what are your talents? Do you like to doodle?

I didn't always have a talent for doodling. It's just something that I've gotten better at with all the moving around we've done. Up North I was more of a talker. I was a good joke teller and I could always make people laugh. Every teacher seemed to know about my talent for talking on the first day. I'd just sit down at my desk and be quietly checking in with my neighbor, when a voice would boom from the front of the room, "Gene Tucks! Is that you I hear?"

But I'm not the way I was Up North, at least not at school. Now, when I do open my mouth, it's usually something really stupid that comes out. So I've become less of a talker and more of a doodler. That way I'm not messing up all the time.

I also have a talent for daydreaming. At least that's what my teacher and parents say. So I guess you could say that I'm multi-talented. I can doodle and I can daydream.

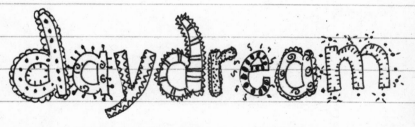

Right now I'm telling you about myself, only I have no idea who you are. I don't even know if you're a boy or a girl. You could be anyone.

Did you get to choose which journal you got, or did your teacher just plop this one down on your desk?

I'll talk to you later,
Gene Tucks, 6th Grade

Sept. 15th

The Last Prompt

Dear Toni,
    Today is the last day that Mr. Mackenzie is giving us a prompt. We're supposed to write about our families. This is really going to bore you to death!

Sorry,
Gene

I Wish We Were Rich But We're Not

My family isn't poor, but we're definitely not rich. We rent our apartment and we own our car. But then, owning a car that my dad got for two hundred fifty dollars from the auto wreckers isn't *really* owning a car. It's more like we own bits and pieces of three or four different cars. This explains the red door on the passenger side and the front fender that's green when most of the car is brown. Dad says that he'll have it looking like it rolled off the lot in no time. It's been about two years, and we're still driving around in a car that seriously needs a paint job. If for some reason our rust bucket is still running, and things haven't improved in our family, I'll be riding around in bits and pieces of a sixty-five-year-old wreck when you read this. It's one of the drawbacks of having a dad who can fix just about anything.

My mom's name is Carol and my dad's name is Larry. I have one brother who's nine. Mom and Dad call him Drew; I call him "The Fly."

We don't have any pets because the landlady won't let us have a dog or cat, and my mom is petrified of rodents. *Petrified* is our vocabulary word today. The interesting thing about the word *petrified* is that it can mean "really scared of something," or like "really old trees that have turned into rocks." So, if it really is forty years into the future and you're reading my journal, it just might be petrified!

I told you that my family history would be boring.
Gene

PS

I hope you like my doodles. This is our car, and the kid in the back with a bag over her head is me. The other kid, with his head hanging out the window like a dog on vacation, is The Fly. I don't really put a bag over my head, but I never look out the window when we go anywhere, especially now that the wreck has started to rust.

I'll bet you've got a really cool car that flies or something. I'd love to go for a ride in it!!!!!

Sept. 18th

My Life Is Over

Dear Toni,

It all began last night with my hair, and then the next thing I knew I was missing my bangs.

"You need a haircut," my mom snarled. "Your bangs are almost down to your nose." I just knew it. She was going to try to convince my dad to cut my hair. I say *try*, because the last time Dad cut my hair he sliced my ear. As far as he's concerned, my bangs can grow all the way to China, because he's not going to cut my hair ever again, especially after the scene I made at the hospital when I found out I needed a stitch.

What happened next is what millions of kids should fear. After banishing The Fly to his room (that was the good part), Mom took out a comb, her very sharp scissors, and her latest flea-market find — electric dog clippers!

I have a very ticklish neck and electric dog clippers buzzing around my face and dropping billions of little hair bits down onto my nose created a very dangerous scenario. I sneezed and my mom jumped and buzzed off half my bangs.

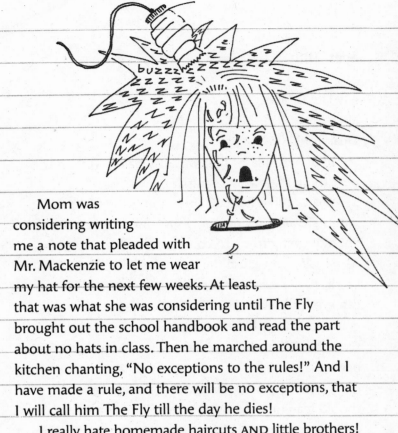

Mom was
considering writing
me a note that pleaded with
Mr. Mackenzie to let me wear
my hat for the next few weeks. At least,
that was what she was considering until The Fly
brought out the school handbook and read the part
about no hats in class. Then he marched around the
kitchen chanting, "No exceptions to the rules!" And I
have made a rule, and there will be no exceptions, that
I will call him The Fly till the day he dies!

I really hate homemade haircuts AND little brothers!

Your very stupid-looking pen pal,
Gene Tucks

The Door Mat that Was Me

I did a pretty good job of racing unnoticed to the school. Unfortunately, I hit the first two steps of the school stairs with my knees and plowed directly into the third with my chest. Then I watched, as hundreds of stampeding 3rd Graders rumbled up the steps. My brand-new, three-ringed binder sailed through the air, and I am sure that ten thousand kids wiped their feet on my homework.

Mr. Mackenzie picked me up off the front steps and suggested that I tie my shoelaces to prevent further injury. So, when I arrived late for class, he only lifted his eyebrows over his wire-rimmed glasses and nodded.

I'll write more later. It's already time to put away our journals.

Your pen pal with two left feet and no brain,
Gene Tucks

PS
No one seems to have noticed my lack of bangs, but then, no one has really noticed that I'm here at all.
Maybe I should be signing my journal,
Invisible Gene

Sept. 19th

Dear Toni,
    I spent most of recess reading over my journal.
I've decided that it's probably a good idea to make
sure that all of my sentences begin with capitals
and that I don't have too many run-ons. That's
what Mr. Mackenzie wrote on my other writing
assignment.

Lunch

Mr. Mackenzie asked me to stay for a few minutes
before lunch. He asked how things were going with
my new classmates. I told him things were great.
I know that's a lie, but I also know, from all my
moving around, that friends are never made by
having the teacher feel sorry for you. He told me that
Harry Gray had a girls' field-hockey team. I've never
played or even seen field hockey, but it sounds like
fun. He also said that I might be working too hard on
my writing project. I guess I'm supposed to write to
you at home after I finished my homework, during
free writing in the morning, or when I'm finished my
work in class; not at recess and lunch. So, I guess I'll be

writing to you a bit less at school. Don't worry, though.
I won't forget about you!

Your pen pal,
Gene Tucks

Sept. 20th

A Grove of Maples

Dear Toni,
    Our class planted thirty-two maple seedlings
along the walkway to our school today. If we take
care of them and if the next class and the next class
water them, in forty years you will be able to come
and see the trees that we planted for you. Right now,
I'm a lot taller than they are, but I think they'll be
over fifty feet tall by the time you come to this school.
Mr. Mackenzie told us that when he was in Grade 6,
his class planted a hundred maple trees in a park to
celebrate Canada's one hundredth birthday. Now,
whenever he goes back to his hometown he sees the
giant trees. He said that every Christmas Eve, a bunch
of his friends meet in that park for a game of hockey.
Now that would be fun!

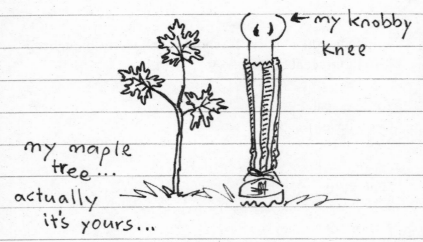

← my knobby knee

my maple tree...
actually it's yours...

(the 11th one from the street)

Gene

PS
I planted the eleventh tree from the street. Eleven is my lucky number! What's yours?

Sept. 21st

We've Got Money!

You heard it first, Toni,
MY DAD'S GOT A MECHANIC JOB!!!!!! It's at the same place as his part-time job, only now he's their

mechanic! Like I said, he can fix just about anything. Well, anything with an engine, but unfortunately not my bangs, which are now sticking straight out from my head like a baseball cap brim.

MY DAD GOT A MECHANIC JOB!

Today, my dad picked my brother and me up from school and took us for an "any size" ice cream at King Cream. I hope King Cream will still be around when you're a kid. It's the best place to go for ice cream – the large size at King Cream is twice as big as an ice cream anywhere else for the same price!

Dad said now that he's got regular work, we might be able to find a place of our own and settle down.

There are a few places at the Silver Star Trailer Court for sale, and he and Mom are thinking about going to look at them. The place is loaded with kids, which would be great because I'm sick of playing with The Fly all the time.

The other thing is, that our apartment building is full of people who want you to be quiet. Well, everybody except for Mrs. Creole. She loves all the noise that The Fly and I make. But I'm not so sure she actually hears everything we are saying. Most of the time when I'm chasing my brother, I'm trying to kill him, and he's screaming for my mom or dad. Well, not really *kill* him, but you know, get even.

Living in the trailer court would be so much better! I'd have kids for neighbors! Not that you aren't a good friend, Toni. It's just that I would kind of like someone I could hang out with or stay over with at their house on the weekends. You understand, right?

Your soon-to-have-a-room-of-her-own friend,
Gene Tucks

Sept. 22nd

School Goals

Dear Toni,

Mr. Mackenzie has been talking to us about setting goals. Adults always want kids to set goals that make them better students or tidier people. But I was thinking that my big goal for Grade 6 is to find a really good friend. I haven't had a best friend since we left Pelican Lake, and I'd like one. Especially now that it looks like we'll be staying around here for awhile. My other goal is to make the field-hockey team. Practices start tomorrow. I'm sure I can get to know some cool kids if I make the team.

On the little sheet of paper that we all had to tape to our desks with our goals written on them I wrote, *Try not to daydream*, and *Keep up with my homework*. Both goals I know my parents would like. But my real goals, which only you will know, are to find a good friend and to make the field-hockey team!

Do you have any goals for the year?

Bye for now,
Gene

24

PS
Field hockey is a lot like hockey, except there's no ice.
(You play on grass.)

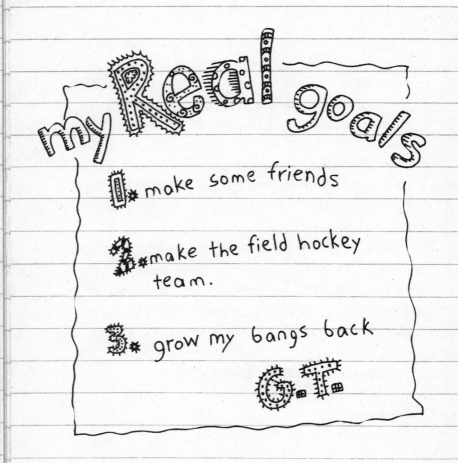

my Real goals

1. make some friends

2. make the field hockey
   team.

3. grow my bangs back

G.T.

Sept. 23rd

The Silver Star Is Not Too Far

Dear Toni,

   Mom and Dad went to look at a trailer today.
Mom said The Fly and I couldn't go because we'd fall
in love with the place right away and be pressuring
them to buy it. So, I'm stuck baby-sitting. I sure hope
the trailer court allows dogs. I'd love to have a dog of
my own. None of the places we've rented since we
moved from Pelican Lake have allowed dogs. Do you
own a dog?

Future Resident of the Silver Star Trailer Park,
Gene Tucks

YES!!!!!!!

Mom and Dad like the trailer! The Fly and I get to go
tomorrow and have a look. I'll tell you more when I
get home.

Life is great!
Gene

Sept. 24th

The Trailer Is Great!

Dear Toni,

    The trailer isn't new, but Mom says if we get it, The Fly and I can paint our rooms however we want. There's a skinny door that goes from my room into the bathroom. Mom is hoping it will encourage a bit more bathing. There's a long hall and The Fly thinks it's perfect for car racing.

    Best of all, there's a yard. I saw a miniature poodle a few trailers down, so I'm positive that dogs are ALLOWED. I asked about getting a dog, but Mom just says we'll see, and she's got enough on her plate right now. At least she didn't say no. If the bank approves our loan, the place will be ours!

Your dog-shopping friend,
Gene Tucks

PS
I've been thinking that maybe I'll start a dog-walking business. That way, I can buy my own dog if Mom and Dad say no.

Sept. 25th

Field Hockey Begins!!!!!

Dear Toni,

 We have field-hockey practices every day this week
after school. It looks like everyone has played before,
and they all seem to know each other. I hope I make
the team! Not only would it be fun, it would also
mean I'd have something to do after school.

Gene

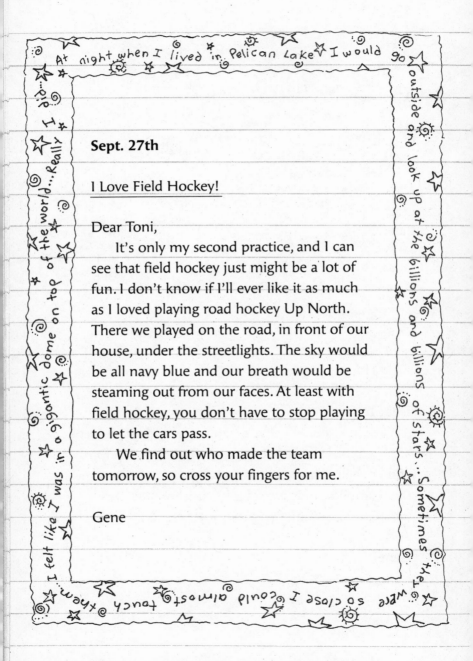

At night when I lived in Pelican Lake I would go outside and look up at the billions and billions of stars... Sometimes they were so close I could almost touch them. I felt like I was in a gigantic dome on top of the world... Really did I

Sept. 27th

I Love Field Hockey!

Dear Toni,

   It's only my second practice, and I can see that field hockey just might be a lot of fun. I don't know if I'll ever like it as much as I loved playing road hockey Up North. There we played on the road, in front of our house, under the streetlights. The sky would be all navy blue and our breath would be steaming out from our faces. At least with field hockey, you don't have to stop playing to let the cars pass.

   We find out who made the team tomorrow, so cross your fingers for me.

Gene

Sept. 28th

Good News, Bad News

Good news Toni!

I made the field-hockey team, and I got my lucky number — eleven! The bad news is, we got our team uniforms, and you won't believe it, but the uniforms are T-shirts and SKIRTS! How will I ever bend over and pick up the ball? Are we supposed to curtsy or something? We're going to get laughed off the field in these. I'm going to wear my gym strip under the skirt. Who cares if my gym shorts go all the way to my knees? This skirt thing barely covers my underwear!

Part of me wishes I'd never made the team.

too short skirt thing...→

field hockey stick...

knobby knees...

Your ridiculous-looking friend,
Gene

PS

If you don't know what *ridiculous* means, well, it means me in my field-hockey uniform. My knees really are truly this knobby and the skirt really is that short.

Sept. 29th

The Birthday

Dear Toni,

Wow, it's been a big week! I made the field-hockey team, and now I've been invited to a birthday party. The girl's name is Kelty, and she's invited all the girls in 6th Grade. I'd say she is about the most popular kid in our class. It's the first time I've been invited anywhere so far this year. I kind of want to go, and I'm kind of scared to go all at the same time.

At first, I thought that I was the only one who hadn't been invited, but then I found my invitation out by my hook in the hall. There's a number to call to RSVP. I'm going to call as soon as I get home. Just in case you don't know, RSVP is French for "Please call back."

Kelty wrote my name *J-E-A-N* on the envelope. It looks good that way, and I think I'll change how I spell my name – at least in my journal and at school!

Your friend to the end,
Jean Tucks

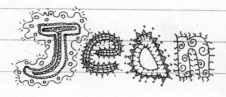

PS
I wish you could RSVP me.

Sept. 30th

Three More Days Until the Party

Dear Toni,

I took all of my allowance and some of my savings and ended up buying Kelty three different presents. The women in the Five and Dime must have asked me a thousand times if I needed help. It's really hard to know what to buy when you don't know the person you're buying for. When I went to pay, she asked if it was my best friend's birthday party that I was going to. I told her it was. I know it's not a good idea to go around lying, but to tell you the truth, it felt great at that moment to have a best friend and to be a best friend. I decided to look up *best friend* in the dictionary when I got home, I couldn't find it but I did find *friend*: "An ally or confidante. Someone who cares about you and someone you confide in that is not a relative." Well I guess that makes you about the only friend I have right now.

It's not that I've never had a friend. I have. I had a best friend until Grade 3. Her name was Brenda and our parents were friends before we were even born. In fact, all my friends Up North were kids whose parents were friends with my parents. I'd never really had to go out and *make* new friends until we moved.

In Pelican Lake, we were all so glad to have another kid around that we fought over who could play with the new kid. Believe me, things are different here. Mom says that it's difficult for her and Dad also. They grew up in Pelican Lake and went to school with a lot of their friends.

But here, every time the telephone rings, the three

of us just look at each other and yell for The Fly.
It's always for him.

So I hope it's okay if I call you my friend,
Jean

PS
I hope you don't think I'm a liar because I lied about
the friend thing today. I'm not, really.

PPS
When's your birthday?

Oct. 2nd

She Shoots! She scores!

Dear Toni,
    You won't believe it. I scored a goal in our first field-
hockey game today! It was just a practice game, but it
looks like those road-hockey skills are coming in handy.
I wish you could have been there to see it. It was great!
It wasn't the winning goal or anything, but it was a
goal. The coach says that she can tell I've played a lot

of hockey by the way I handle my stick. One thing
for sure; it's a lot easier to run when it's not thirty
below zero.

Two of the girls on my team came up and
crossed sticks with me. Tracy, our team captain,
was one of them.

From #11 on the Harry Gray Hawks,
J.T.

PS
In the end, it wasn't as embarrassing as I thought. The
other team had the same ridiculous skirts on. So there
we all were, flapping around the field. My coach said
that the extra long shorts were a little much, but when
I told her that I'd never worn a skirt before, she just
smiled and shrugged her shoulders.

Oct. 3rd

Wasted Money
_____

Dear Toni,

You won't believe it. First of all, I didn't know that
we were NOT supposed to bring presents. What does

someone with their own swimming pool, tennis court, and gigantic, humongous house need from me, Rental Jean? That's what Kelty's friend Julia called me, anyway.

Kelty was nice about the gifts, but I felt like the dumbest person on the planet. How did I read that invitation a hundred thousand times and not read the part about no gifts? On top of all that, I spent all my allowance and half of my savings on gifts that I wasn't even suppose to buy.

I never did get a chance to talk much with Kelty — her *best friends* were with her all the time.

Then Dad left home before I could call and stop him from picking me up from the party. So there I was, getting into our rust bucket, when Kelty came out to say good-bye. Julia was laughing and pointing at us.

I wish Dad would just drive our junk-mobile back to the wreckers where it belongs.

Gene

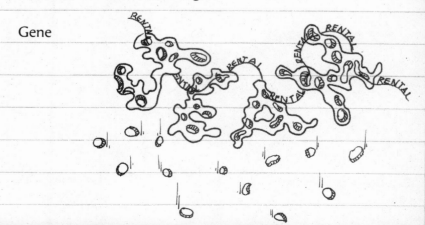

PS
I've decided that I don't want to change the way I spell
my name. It's probably a good idea to stick with a
name that means something because Jean just sounds
like *Rental* Jean now.

Oct. 4th

Nothing to Write About

Dear Toni,

   I'm sure that everyone knows about the present
thing and the wreck. We still haven't heard anything
back from the bank about the trailer loan. When I
grow up, I am going to make a lot of money. That way,
I can just buy whatever I want!

Gene

Oct. 5th

A Letter from Brenda

Dear Toni,

    I got a letter from Brenda Burel today. She's my best friend from Up North. Her mom says hi, and that they all miss my silly jokes. I haven't told anyone in my class a joke yet this year. I don't even know if I remember any.

    Everything is great Up North. They've already had their first snowfall and snowball-making is in full gear every lunch hour. When I lived Up North, I used to think that it would be great to live someplace where it didn't always snow on Halloween. Now I'd give anything to be there. Brenda says everyone still talks about our family's annual Halloween party. It was so much fun. After trick-or-treating, half the town would come over to our house. Mom and Dad always built a bonfire and made hot chocolate. The parents would sit around the fire, and all the kids would head into our living room. According to my dad, the trading that happened in our living room on Halloween night was second only to the NHL draft. Those were the best days, the best house, and the best friends a kid could have. Not like here.

Gene Tucks

Oct. 6th

Field-Hockey Practice

Dear Toni,
     I like practice and being part of a team. But it's the only part I like about being here.

Gene

Oct. 7th

Mom and Dad Are Mad!

Dear Toni,
     Yep, they sure are. Mom is hardly talking to anyone. Most of all she is not talking to my dad other than to say, "I am not interested in talking about it!" On these kinds of days, The Fly and I just go to our rooms and wait for the storm to pass. That's what my dad always says. "Not to worry. This storm will pass soon enough." I'm beginning to wonder, this has been one heck of a long storm. I wish that when adults argued, they'd let the kids know what they are arguing about. I always think it's about me.

Gene

Found a Letter!

I know that I'm not supposed to open mail that's addressed to someone else, but I just couldn't help it. A letter came from the bank today, and it was going to be hours before Mom and Dad got home. I steamed it open. I'd seen that on a detective show and it really works. After it dried I just put a little glue on the sealed part, and, other than it being a little bit wavy, you could hardly tell it had been opened.

The best part is that the bank has APPROVED our loan. I'll bet this is what my parents have been arguing about. But that will ALL change now! Life is about to get better!!!!!

.... suppose to be a detective hat...

I don't actually have one though..

Your *Super Sleuth* pen pal,
Gene

What the Heck is Going ON????

I don't get it. I know that Mom has seen the letter
because I gave it to her myself. She just set it back on
the counter after she read it. I asked her if it was good
news, but she said that it didn't really matter what the
bank said, because my dad has other plans.

From your friend who never will understand adults,
Gene

Oct. 9th

Thanksgiving Dinner

Dear Toni,
    Today is Thanksgiving. Mr. Mackenzie told us
on Friday that we might want to tell you about the
things we are thankful for in our lives. I decided to
make a list.
Number 1   I am thankful that my mom and dad are
still married . . . although that may not be for long.
Number 2   I am thankful that I am writing to you,
and that I have at least one friend in my life . . . that
would be you.

<u>Number 3</u> I'm thankful for turkey dinner, with gravy and mashed potatoes and cranberries . . . even if it is just going to be my brother, my mom, me, and Dad. And maybe Mrs. Creole if she's not gone to be with her kids.

Thankfully yours,
Gene

PS
Oh yeah, and I am thankful that the bank approved our loan for the trailer . . . Now, if my mom and dad will just start talking. . . . Last but not least, I would be extremely thankful for a dog of my own.

Oct. 10th

Confession Time

Dear Toni,

Mom's decided that we're going to visit my grandma for a couple of days. "We" doesn't include my dad. Maybe my parents are getting a divorce. I've decided to tell Mom and Dad about the envelope steaming and all of the other sneaky stuff I've done.

I have a history of peeking at Christmas presents and lying about homework. It's all going to STOP. And I'm going to promise to be more helpful and less of a bother. I mean it! I'm even going to quit asking about getting a dog. Well, maybe I won't quit asking about the dog. But I will try being nicer to The Fly. And that is no easy task.

Your friend who is not looking forward to the future,
Gene

Oct. 11th

The Hardest Day of My Life

Dear Toni,
 I think today has been the hardest day of my life. I have felt sick all day, and now it's only minutes until my mom and dad get home and I tell them about all my lies. You might be thinking, *Why does Gene think she is the reason that her parents aren't speaking to each other?* Well, most of the arguments my parents have are about me. The last time they argued, my mom said that I was driving a wedge between her and Dad. Maybe that's what has happened. Maybe I am the

reason they are arguing. What if it's too late and they've already decided to get a divorce?

The Wedge,
Gene

Time To Tell the Truth

Well, I did it. I told Mom and Dad about the envelope steaming and about last year's Christmas present peek. Once I started talking, all the lies I've told to everyone I've ever known, just started pouring out of me like milk out of a jug.

Then before I knew it I was down on the floor pleading with my parents not to get a divorce. I can't believe I've actually told that many lies in just eleven years. Well, maybe only ten years, because I don't think I lied before I could talk.

Dad says he hopes I put my vivid imagination to work and start figuring out how I am going to save myself from myself. "A conscience," he says, "is your best friend and your worst enemy. You don't want to get on the wrong side of it." I think for once he might be right.

Anyway, the best thing is that after I peeled myself off my dad's knees, my parents sat down with The Fly and me and told us not to worry about a divorce. Then they went out to Burger Barn to talk things through. Mom made Kraft Dinner for The Fly and me, and Mrs. Creole is going to check in on us. Hopefully, she won't come in and watch TV because I just know that The Fly will have to tell her the whole story about today.

Until later,
Gene Tucks

Oct. 12th

I've Been Waiting All Night!

Dear Toni,

I waited for Mom and Dad until 8:30 p.m., expecting that they would tell me what they talked about. Then I was really disappointed when they told me that they were going to sleep on their decision and talk to me in the morning.

Well, I never slept. It's now 5:48 a.m., and they're still not up and I can't sleep. I WANT TO KNOW WHAT THE HECK IS GOING ON!!!!!!! Am I going to get a room of my own and a dog, or not? On top of all that, we are going to visit my grandparents in four days,

and I need to know just what is going on BEFORE
we go!

Your extremely patient pen pal,
Gene

Once Again I Get All the Blame

Well, my mom and dad are not dead, and I am lucky
to be alive. Seems Dad thought I yelled something
about a fire when I gave him a little shake. I remember

thinking about a fire, but I'm sure that I didn't yell "FIRE!"

Mom was steaming mad and said that we should just get ourselves dressed quietly and talk after school. She says I'm to blame for the wait. The Fly really went all out: crying about being ripped from his bed and frightened to death, when my dad carried him down the fire escape and onto the front lawn. At least that's what Mom and Dad saw. What they didn't see was his pesky, smirking face all happy that I, once again, was getting into trouble.

Your friend who gets all the blame, just like I told you!
Gene Tucks

I Just Wanted to Say Hi

Sometimes I wonder what life will be like in forty years. Maybe you could write back to me and tell me what it's like to be a kid. That would be great. But I guess we'll have to talk about that later because Mr. Mackenzie is forcing me to go outside without my journal these days. I don't see why. All I do is stand around alone. Mr. Mackenzie says he figures that my writing is definitely going to improve, considering the amount of time I spend on the journal project. It's just that I still don't really know the kids in my class. You're the kid I know best. I don't even want to be friends with anyone else. They would all probably call me Rental Jean anyway.

Gene

Oct. 13th

Bikes

Dear Toni,

There are two types of kids in this school. Rich kids, who all hang out together and admire each other's fancy bikes, some of which are worth — no, *all* of which are worth more than our car. The rest of the kids stand around and wish the rich kids' expensive bikes belonged to them. Some days it seems like they've made some kind of bet as to who can ignore me the longest.

Sorry if I sound like a whiner. I'm not really. But I'm also not doing very well on my first goal.

Stuck nowhere,
Gene

Oct. 14th

FINALLY a Dream Come True!!!!!!!

So here it goes, Toni,

This is what my parents have been arguing about. My dad's boss down at the gas station has offered our family free rent in the empty apartment at back of the station, in exchange for managing the place while he and his wife are away on holidays.

My dreams are coming TRUE!!!!!!!! There is an A-frame cottage in the backyard, and you're never going to believe what they use it for. I'll bet you can't guess. . . .

Okay, okay! I'll tell you. . . . It's a doghouse for a giant St. Bernard and her three pups. And guess who gets to take care of them? You got it! ME!!!!!

This is where Mom and I disagree. She is sure that it's too much responsibility, and that she'll end up out there "Picking up dog poop!" (She didn't say poop, but I probably shouldn't tell you what she said.)

I know she's wrong and being a pessimist (*pessimist* was one of our vocabulary words this week) about it – she's expecting the worst.

Dad says: "I'd love to give it a try. What do we have to lose?"

I said: "Nothing!"

The Fly said: "A room of my own!"

Mom said: "My sanity!"

But in the end, we decided to go for it, and I think it's going to be great! We get to move in on the 23rd of October because no one is in the place now, and our landlady has found someone to rent our apartment. I guess Halloween won't be so bad after all.

The other great part is, we all get to help out in the gas station. The bad part is, Mom thinks that if we don't buy the trailer now, someone else will, and who knows when another one will come along that we can afford. Dad is sure that we'll be able to save a whack of money living at the gas station. His boss has said that if it works out, we can stay there for as long as we want.

Mom keeps saying that the gas station apartment is about the size of a shoebox, and any money we save will probably be spent on funerals. She is sure we'll end up killing each other in such close quarters.

Dad keeps repeating that he is sure we'll be able to save a whack of money and get back on our feet. He also thinks it will be a great experience for The Fly and me. I agree with him!

Your pen pal who is about to start living her dream,
Gene

We're Leaving

Tomorrow morning we leave for Pelican Lake to visit my grandparents. I get to miss two days of school. My coach is letting me take a field-hockey stick, ball, and uniform to show Brenda. It's going to be a long drive, but it will be great to go and visit my grandparents and all my friends at my old school. I hope they remember me. I'm taking you with me! How about that, you get to go on a road trip!

Let's get packing.
Gene

Oct. 15th

Kid Abuse!!!!

Dear Toni,
    The drive is taking forever, and I'm one of those kids who can't sleep when I'm traveling. I'm sure it would go a lot faster if Mom would stop in restaurants to eat. But no, she makes bologna, ketchup, and mustard sandwiches. Don't get me wrong. I like

bologna sandwiches, but I'd rather have fries
and gravy.

The worst thing is needing to go to the bathroom.
If there's no gas station in sight, my mom will make
you get out of the car and run through the ditch to a
tiny little bush and pee there. I think it should be
against the law for parents to make kids pee at the side
of the road. The Fly thinks it's no big deal, but he has
no idea how it is for a girl!

I'll write more later. . . .

Gene

Later. . . .

It was dark when we finally got to my grandma's,
but we're here, and Mom has promised to get me up
early, so I can catch the bus to school tomorrow. I've
got to get some sleep: only six hours till I catch the
school bus.

It's good to be Home Sweet Home.
Gene

52

Oct. 16th

Back in My Old School

Dear Toni,

Here you and I are in my old school. Mr. Ferance
(he would be my teacher if we still lived here) said
that I could just do my journal writing, instead of the
work they are doing. It was great to walk up the stairs
and know where everything was. Every time one of
the teachers goes by they say "Hello," and ask me
where we're living. I keep wanting to say that we've
moved back.

A lot of other families have left, but there are still
kids I know in my class. I told them we were going to
be living in the back of a gas station, and that I get
to take care of a St. Bernard and her pups. Brenda's
lived her whole life on a farm, and she thinks it would
be neat to have people driving up into your yard all the
time. Oh yeah, and Brenda says "Hi!"

Being at my old school is so different from being
at my new school. Here, everyone knows me and
likes me.

I hear Mom telling people that things are going
well and we're finally starting to get back on our feet. It

feels good when I hear her say that. It feels like everything is going to be okay.

Tomorrow you and I are going to stay over at Brenda's house. I can't wait.

Gene

Oct. 17th

Cinnamon Sugar Butter Toast!

Dear Toni,

It's great to stay at Brenda's! I woke up early and went down to the kitchen. Brenda's mom, Sue, was already in from doing the chores, so we sat down at the table and chewed the fat. That's what Sue calls having a real person-to-person talk.

The thing I like about Sue is that she really is interested in how things are going, but she doesn't ask a bunch of questions. Sue says "Hi, from forty years ago!" She'll be almost eighty years old when you get this journal.

The other thing that's really great about Sue is that she makes the best cinnamon sugar butter toast in the whole world. She gave me two loaves of homemade bread and a jar of her Secret-Recipe Cinnamon Sugar to take back. The Fly will weep when I tell him the whole jar is for me!

It's been great to be here. At least I'll have the dogs at the gas station when I get home.

Gene

PS
My grandma and grandpa are going to visit us in December. Grandma told me that they'll stay in a hotel with a swimming pool and restaurant. Then The Fly and I can stay with them for the whole weekend!

Oct. 18th

The Drive Home

Dear Toni,

I hope that you never have to endure a drive over a mountain pass without a heater in your car. I thought it would never end. *Endure* was one of our vocabulary words before I left, and I can definitely tell Mr. Mackenzie that I know exactly what it means!

The heater in the wreck quit halfway home, and we nearly froze to death going over the mountain pass. The only good thing about the entire trip was that Mom was forced to stop at restaurants for fries and gravy and hot chocolate so that we could warm up. When we'd get back into the wreck, she'd scrape the inside of the windshield so that we could see out of it. I was sure my toes were going to fall off from frostbite. The guy at the gas station said that he couldn't repair the heater. Mom said that it was probably a good thing he couldn't, because it would have cost an arm and a leg, and Dad could fix it for free when we got home. So instead, the arms and legs that it almost cost were mine!

We are all going over to the Lees' gas station tomorrow after supper. I can't wait!

Your pen pal, who crossed a mountain pass in a car so old, it could be called a covered wagon.
Gene

Oct. 19th

The Shoebox

Dear Toni
Well, I'm back at school and it isn't too bad.
I've got to pack up my room this week, and Mom
wants me to be really picky about everything I plan
to bring to the shoebox. That's what she calls our new
apartment at the station. I told her that if she keeps
calling it a shoebox, everyone is going to think she is
the "old woman who didn't know what to do!" I guess
I'll just put all my Halloween costumes in storage
because I can't imagine there will be any bonfires or
friends to trade candy with at the gas station.

Gene

Oct. 20th

The Dogs are Amazing!

Dear Toni,
We move in three days! I can't wait. The pups and
Sally (that's the mother dog) are so cute. There are

three pups. Two are normal size and one is a runt. They kind of look like this and they kind of don't . . . it's not easy drawing three squirmy puppies. The one with the big black spot on her face is Lucy. She's the biggest and the softest. The pup with one brown ear and one white ear is Shady. The little guy is Boxer. Note his very stubby nose and brown paw! Mr. Lee says they'll weigh more than I do now when they're full grown. Yikes!

I love them already and I'm packing like crazy!
Gene

BOXER

Shady

LUCY

SALLY

Oct. 21st

Dinner with Mrs. Creole

Dear Toni,
    Mrs. Creole had our family over for supper tonight.
She's been a great neighbor! She gave me a book on
dogs and The Fly a new baseball cap as a going away
present. Mom told her that we're not going that far,
and we'll have her over for Sunday dinner. That would
be nice, because Mrs. Creole is like a grandma to
The Fly and me. Besides, she doesn't have any family
nearby.

Bye for now,
Gene

Check Out Receipt

Orange Terrace Library
951-826-2184
www.riversideca.gov/library

Saturday, September 16, 2017
11:19:38 AM
12884

Item: 0000130782980
Title: Next spring an oriole
Call no.: J WHELAN
Due: 09/30/2017

Item: 0000144398203
Title: The grave robber's apprentice
Call no.: J STRATTON
Due: 09/30/2017

Item: 0000142068923
Title: DEAR TONI
Call no.: J SAND-EVELAND
Due: 09/30/2017

Total items: 3

You just saved $28.89 by using your
library. You have saved $28.89 this
past year and $51.79 since you began
using the library!

Thank You!

AR BookFind.com
Student

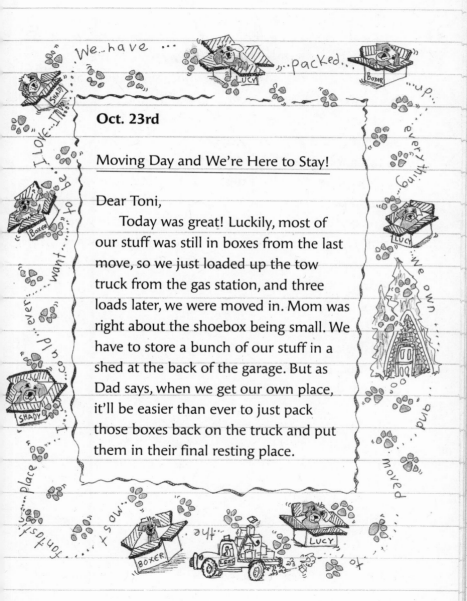

Oct. 23rd

Moving Day and We're Here to Stay!

Dear Toni,

Today was great! Luckily, most of our stuff was still in boxes from the last move, so we just loaded up the tow truck from the gas station, and three loads later, we were moved in. Mom was right about the shoebox being small. We have to store a bunch of our stuff in a shed at the back of the garage. But as Dad says, when we get our own place, it'll be easier than ever to just pack those boxes back on the truck and put them in their final resting place.

I really don't care about sharing a room with The Fly. I'm planning to spend most of my time in the doghouse with the dogs. The doghouse is really a cabin that is shaped like a Swiss chalet, and it's the perfect home for Sally and her pups. There's also a great campground that's empty right now, and behind that, there's a forest with gigantic cedar trees.

The poop thing isn't near as bad as my mom said it would be, the pups are only two weeks old, and Sally cleans up their messes all by herself, if you know what I mean. There's a cozy bed for the dogs in the corner of the main floor. The puppies can't climb over the sides, and Sally isn't interested in anything else but taking care of them.

The Fly has been busy learning how to wash windshields. I sure hope we don't lose a bunch of customers because of the mess he makes of all their windows.

Your very happy friend,
Gene

Oct. 26th

Dogs Are a Girl's Best Friend

Dear Toni,

I'm sorry I didn't write to you for a few days. We had a substitute teacher, and she made us hand in our journals when it took so long for everyone to settle down after the bell. Then, she made us sit with our heads down until we were all quiet. I'm sure you know how the substitute thing works. I just sat there and watched. By the end of her stint, I think Ms. Elliot was about ready to quit teaching.

My first week in the shoebox has been really busy and very wonderful. The pups are amazing. All I want to do is live in the doghouse and watch them play. They climb all over me when I lie on the floor. Sometimes I think I might have made a better dog than a kid.

People say a dog is a man's best friend. A dog, Toni, is a girl's best friend too! So many times when I was in the A-frame I kept thinking, *I have to tell Toni about this, I have to tell Toni about that.*

It is just so cool to be with the dogs, I love them. I'm sure you would too. Even if you didn't like dogs before, I'm sure you would fall in love with these puppies. They are the cutest things I have ever seen!

Mr. Lee left me a book to keep notes about the pups. He said it will help me remember to do the feeding and cleaning up. Caring for the dogs is a lot of responsibility. But I love it!!!!!

Happy days are here again!
Gene

Oct. 27th

The Fly Is a Thief and He's Been Caught!

Dear Toni,

The Fly, other than making a mess of people's windshields, is not really that much help here at the gas station. He can't run the till (because he can't count back change), and my mom says that pumping gas is too dangerous. But that's not the only thing. The Fly has been caught stealing chocolate bars. Mom gave me the same talk she gave him about stealing. I may have snuck a few bars, but I have paid for all of them.

Your pen pal who is not a thief.
Gene Tucks

Oct. 28th

New Kid in the Neighborhood. . . . Yay!

Dear Toni,

   I think I told you about the campground next to the gas station. It was closed down for the winter, but my dad has agreed to let a woman and her kid park there for a few weeks. Dad says that they have camped there before, during the summer, and he is sure that Mr. Lee wouldn't mind them being there.

   The new kid and her mom live in an old school bus that has flowers painted all over the sides. The mom's an artist who sells her stuff at craft fairs and music festivals. They travel around in their bus all the time. I'm going over to meet them after supper. I hope the kid likes hanging out in a doghouse. It's going to be great to have a friend right next door. I wonder where she is from. Maybe we'll be able to walk to school together.

Winnifred Spencer

Well, Toni, I met the new kid. Her name is Winnifred
Spencer, and she's about the same age as me . . . I
think. I started to tell her about Sally and the pups, but
she already knows Sally. I guess Mr. Lee lets her hang
out with Sally during the summers, when she and her
mom camp here. Anyway, this might sound kind of
strange, but at first I was really excited about meeting
her, and now that I have, I'm not. I was just starting to
feel like Sally and the pups were mine, but when the
kid came into the doghouse, Sally went wild. She
started *woof-woofing* and, even though the pups
were nursing, she got up and wagged her whole body
over to the kid. Then Winnifred said, "Hey there, Sally,
do you want a hug?" And it sure looked like Sally did.
She sat down and tucked her nose up under the kid's
chin and the kid petted Sally's back. They just sat
there for a long time. It feels like the kid came over and
stole Sally away from me and the puppies. I don't like
her and I don't want her to come back. The Fly says
it's because I'm jealous. I told him I wasn't . . . but
maybe I am.

It would be great if you could come over, Toni,
Gene

Oct. 29th

No Visitors Please!

Dear Toni,

    I put a sign on the door that reads, NO VISITORS!
Dad says Winnifred isn't causing any harm by visiting
the dogs. I disagree! Because when I am plugging away
at school, Winnifred is over
hanging out with my dogs.

I told my dad to watch out for her sneaking over here, but he just said, "What's the matter with that?"

Well, the trouble is that these dogs are my responsibility, and I don't need anyone butting in on my responsibility!

Sorry to be such a grouch.
Gene

I Hate Homework

I'm having a hard time keeping up with my schoolwork. I just want to be with the dogs. I'm supposed to be doing a report on astronomy, but I'm going to ask Mr. Mackenzie if I can do my report on St. Bernards. The only problem with asking him is, then he'll know I haven't even started. *EEEEK!*

Gene

Oct. 30th

Dear Toni,

It's Halloween tomorrow and I don't care! All the kids in my class have plans, and it's all that anyone can talk about. No one asked me what I was doing. But so what? I don't care if I go or not. The Fly has been invited out with a bunch of kids from his class.

Mom and Dad are going over to the painted bus for a BBQ with the kid and her mom, and I don't care!

Ho-ho-humbug. Unhappy, horrible Halloween....I wish you were here. We could go out together.

Gene

Oct. 31st

What Day Is It, Anyway?

Dear Toni,

Is it Halloween if you don't dress up and no one comes to the door? Does eating a whole box of mini chocolate bars count? Or does it mean that Halloween never happened?

I hope you never have a Halloween like this one....It's the worst one there ever was.

Gene

Nov. 1st

New Runners

Dear Toni,
    Dad and I went downtown after supper and
bought me some cleats for field hockey. The Fly
gets my old ones. This might be the only good thing
about being the oldest and the biggest. There's just
something great about something new, especially
shoes. I feel like I can run faster and play better.

I hope it's true.
Gene

Another Chance

The kid's mom came over and asked my mom if she
had any idea why I wouldn't let Winnifred come over,
and you won't believe it, but my mom told her that
she thinks I'm jealous about how much Sally likes
Winnifred. That is so, so, so, so untrue. Anyway, Mom
wants me to give her another chance. Then she gave
me this long speech about how dogs can love more

than one person. I don't know if your parents do this, but when my parents want me to do something, they keep at me until I'm left with two choices.

1. Do what they want.

Or

2. Do what they want.

So guess what . . . I have to do what they want, and that means going to the bus and asking the kid if she'd like to come over.

Gene

Nov. 2nd

Dog-Walking Disaster! Well, Not Really.

Dear Toni,

Winnifred said she wouldn't do the Hey-Sally-do-you-want-a-hug? thing anymore, when I told her that it's really not a good idea to hug dogs. Especially dogs that don't belong to you (and I did read that in a book on dogs). So, I told her if she could follow that rule she could come over, but only when I'm here.

Anyway, I braided a piece of rope into a leash so we could take Sally for a walk. Winnifred was sure that Sally had a harness for walking, but I told her that Mr. Lee hadn't said anything to me about a harness, so we used the rope. The dog walking, if you want to call it that, was hilarious! The puppies wanted to scramble ahead, and Sally got tangled in the leash because she wanted to sniff their butts. Winn was bent over, trying to get a photograph of them and she tripped on the rope. We all ended up in a big puddle on the ground. The dogs were in a knot on top of us, licking our faces and biting our noses. I haven't laughed that hard for a long time.

My gut still hurts from all that laughing.
Bye for now,
Gene

PS
Winnifred says it's okay if I call her Winn.

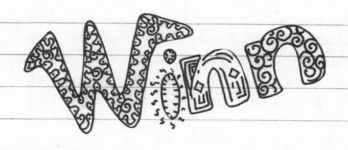

Nov. 3rd

Pictures of Sally

Dear Toni,

   Today when Winn saw me writing down facts for my science project, she told me that she had pictures from when Sally was just a pup. She has a Polaroid camera that she got from her uncle in Saskatoon for her Royal Birthday. A Royal Birthday is when the age you are turning is the same as the date of your birthday.

It's great to see Sally when she was so little! Isn't she cute?
Gene

To the Beach

Winn's mom, Kathy, asked me if I wanted to go with
her and Winn for the weekend. They go to a place
called Wragg Beach and Winn says that they can park
their bus on the edge of the sand. Sounds great! Dad
was all for me going, but said I needed to make plans
for the dogs with Drew if I was going to leave. I told
Dad that The Fly said he wouldn't take care of the
dogs unless I paid him. My dad said that I should try
calling him by his given name, and maybe he'd do it
for free. But I decided I'd just keep calling him The Fly,
instead of Drew, and pay him the $4.00 (in advance)
that he forced out of me.

I got to sleep
up here in a
teeny tiny little
bed...

purple
velvet
curtains

la casa de los flores

kathy's very
wild hair

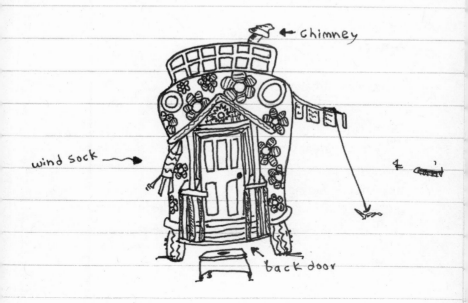

We leave tonight! And I'm bringing you with me. I'll put our journal near the campfire and maybe in forty years you'll still be able to smell the smoke from the burning wood. I love that smell.

Your traveling friend,
Gene

PS
It's such a cool feeling when I think that in forty years you will be here. You're not even born yet and I am talking to you. Mr. Mackenzie said when you are eleven years old, some of us will probably be grandparents. That is such a weird thought! Don't you think?

Nov. 5th

The Great Guitar Weekend!

Dear Toni,

What a great weekend! I feel like I've really been somewhere, even though we were only a couple hours from home. Going in a converted school bus is a really different way to travel and camp. It's beautiful inside, and I think we were the only bus on the road with a woodstove. There are hand-stitched velvet quilts on the couch and on both of the beds. There's a stained-glass window over Winn's bed. It looks like a snow angel. The floors are all smooth and shiny oak planks. It's the kind of home where everything has its own place.

There were two other people camping on the beach, Willow and Genna. They built this neat thing called a sauna that they sat in until they were really hot. After about ten minutes, they came running out from the sauna and dove into the freezing lake. Later they came over to our campsite, and we sat by the fire and sang songs. Both of them brought over drums and they let Winn and me try them. It was fun. Willow said he and Genna are planning on camping on the beach until the summer tourists show up.

This morning we walked on the beach and had a picnic. Kathy showed me a few chords on her guitar, and I actually learned my first song. She's offered to give me lessons while she and Winn are living in the campground. Winn said I could use her guitar. She said she's a lot more interested in photography than learning to play an instrument, which is true, because Winn sure does take a lot of pictures. The thing is, she doesn't really look at people unless they're in a photograph. Then every night, she looks at all the pictures that she packs around in a box. Even when I

talk to her she just kind of looks past me. Anyway,
I don't mean to brag, but Kathy says that I picked up
the guitar quick! Maybe I'll be able to add *musical* to
my rather short list of talents!

Winn let me take some pictures with her camera at
the beach. It's really cool the way it spits them out.

The dogs were glad to see us when we got back.
Sally was really happy to see Winn. She wagged up to
Winn and sat down waiting for Winn to ask her if she
wanted a hug. Winn just patted her on the head and
said goodnight. I wish Sally would come up to me
when I ask her if she wants a hug, but she just acts like
she doesn't understand a word I'm saying.

Bye for now,
Gene

Nov. 7th

Julia the Jerk!

Dear Toni,
Today Winn came to meet me after school. I could
see her waiting outside on the bench. Then Julia and her
gang walked up to Winn and started asking her a bunch

of questions. I could tell by the way they were laughing that they were just making fun of her. I kept waiting for them to leave and Winn kept looking at the school. When I came out the front door, Winn got up off the bench and started walking toward me, but Julia stepped on Winn's long skirt and Winn fell. Julia and the gang laughed and then Julia said, "Gotta be careful there, Hippie Girl, or you'll trip on your rags." I didn't say anything. I just wanted to disappear. Winn got up and I whispered to her that we should get out of there. Julia poked at my jacket just as we walked by and said, "Hey, Rental Jean, is your head itching? Because you know, the last kid who lived in that shack behind the gas station had lice . . . all the time. That place is infested!"

Then Mr. Mackenzie walked by and asked if everything was okay. They all stared at me. I just nodded.

I can't wait for this day to end. I feel sick.
Gene

Teacher Calls Home – Great!#$%&*

Mom got a call from Mr. Mackenzie after school and he told her that I'm having some trouble with some of the kids in my class. I told Mom that everything had been fine until Winn showed up at school. Mom asked what Winn did, but I don't really want to tell her what they said about me living in a shack and about the place being infested with lice. Mom kept on bugging me about what they were saying, so I just told her that they were teasing Winn about living in a bus and me about living at a gas station. Mom said that it's true that the shoebox is not much of a palace, but that we have each other and the dogs. She said, "How many kids can actually have a sleepover with their dogs in the doghouse?" The truth is, I wouldn't trade the fanciest house in the world for my life with the dogs right now.

I just wish my head would stop itching.
Gene

PS
Mr. Mackenzie had us write poems about things that bugged us. I wrote two: one about The Fly and another one about Bedcrumbs. On the top of the Bedcrumbs poem he wrote, "This one is extremely original and, in all my years of teaching, I don't think anyone has ever written about Bedcrumbs. But I'll bet every kid in this class knows

what you're talking about if they've ever eaten toast in bed! Nice job!" Anyway, he thought it would be great if I gave you a copy of my poem, so here it is. It's kind of dumb . . . but it's also kind of true.

Bedcrumbs

Have you ever tried to sleep with
bedcrumbs; I mean bread crumbs
in your bed?

You just nicely get yourself tucked in,
your goodnights are all said.
Then you itch, you itch all over,
from your toes up to your knees,
from your knees up to your elbows,
you feel like you've got fleas.

But it's bedcrumbs; I mean bread crumbs.

And
you can feel them slowly crawling,
you expect that they will bite.
You say, "These thoughts are really stupid."
But they keep you up all night.

Bread crumbs!

Nov. 8th

School Tattletale

Dear Toni,

    Mr. Mackenzie had a talk with the whole class this morning about getting along with each other. At recess, Julia and her gang hissed at me when they walked by. Just what I needed, now I'm a lice-head *and* they think I'm a tattletale on top of everything else. I hate this school and everyone in it!

I just want to move.
Gene

Nov. 9th

Boxer is Sick

Dear Toni,

    One of Sally's pups is sick. It's Boxer, the littlest one. Mom said to wait until morning and, if he isn't any better, we'll take him in to the vet. I asked if I could sleep in the doghouse tonight so that I could keep an eye on him.

I hope Boxer doesn't die.
Gene

Winn to the Rescue

Winn came right over when I asked her, even though she was already in bed. Sally was so glad to see Winn and so were the pups. Even little Boxer tried to pick himself up. I watched Winn as she checked him over to make sure nothing was broken and felt his nose. Winn said she thinks that Boxer isn't getting enough to eat because the other two are always pushing him out of the way, especially now that they are getting so big. Or, she thinks he might have eaten something that's upset his stomach. Winn had me hold Lucy and Shady on my lap, while she convinced Sally to lie down so that Boxer could nurse. She said that Boxer needs to eat first instead of always eating last, because the other two drink all of the milk. I hadn't thought of that. I was just following Mr. Lee's instructions.

After Boxer had eaten all he could eat and fallen asleep, Winn let the other two pups in with Sally. But before Sally laid down she tried to push her nose up under Winn's chin. It was like Sally was saying "Thank you" to Winn, and when Winn just patted her on the head, Sally turned and looked at me.

Gene

Nov. 10th

I Did It! I Stood Up to Julia

Dear Toni,

Well, I woke up this morning and made sure that Boxer got his share of breakfast. Then I went by Winn's and asked if she could take care of him while I was at school. She said she'd go over right away.

This morning on the way into the school, I saw Julia and Kelty. Julia started going on about me tattling to Mr. Mackenzie. Kelty told her to leave me alone, but I just looked at Julia and said, "Call me whatever you want, because what you think means nothing to me." Then The Fly and a group of his friends walked by and, believe it or not, my brother actually stuck up for me. Julia just sneered at them and said, "Whatever."

Gene

Nov. 11th

It's Remembrance Day

Dear Toni,

Today is a day when we are supposed to remember the soldiers who fought in the wars. Mr. Mackenzie said that we should ask our parents or grandparents about WWI and WWII and then write about that. My mom's Uncle Gene (that's the guy I was named after) was in WWII. My mom has a beret that he wore that hangs on a picture of him in our living room. Last night, before I went to bed, I asked Mom if she knew any of his war stories. She said that the only thing he ever told her about the war was "Killing another person is something that you can't ever forget, and you don't ever want to remember."

Mom said that Great-Uncle Gene was only sixteen years old when he enlisted. All his friends who could, enlisted with him. Most of them never came home, and Great-Uncle Gene never really liked to talk about the war.

I hope I never have to go to war and that you never have to either.
Gene

Nov. 12th

Basic Commands

Dear Toni,

Boxer is completely back to his old self. Winn and I have started to work with Sally walking with the rope. Winn even put the huge collar on her own neck, and the two of us paraded around the A-frame, trying to show Sally how it was done. Winn was barking and prancing. I think today was the best day I've had since we moved from Pelican Lake. I have never laughed so hard. Winn even pretended to drink out of Sally's water dish.

The funniest thing was when Winn stood up on her knees and asked for a doggie treat. I couldn't believe it when I dared Winn to eat it, and she did. She says they're great and I should try one.

every dog's favorite treat!
...maybe Winn's too...

YUM YUMS

The problem is that Sally doesn't like to wear a collar. Winn said that we need to put it on her and then distract her until she forgets it's on. It seemed to work. Now Sally is just lying around with it on, like she doesn't even know it's there.

From one half of the dog-training team,
Gene

Nov. 13th

Sleepover Just One Day Away

Dear Toni,

I can't wait. Winn and I are going to have a sleepover in the doghouse. Winn's mom has to go into the hospital for some tests and so Winn is spending the next few days with us.

Winn gets to stay and help out in the gas station with my mom while I'm at school. After school, she and I are going to field-hockey practice. I told her it might be a sport that she would really like. For sure, she'd love the uniforms! Unlike me, Winn only wears skirts.

Gotta go,
Gene

Nov. 14th

Winn's a Rule Book

Dear Toni,

It is so amazing how Winn can read anything and memorize it. She was asking my coach a lot of questions about how the game was played, so my coach gave her a rule book. Winn read it in about ten minutes, and then she told me tons of things I didn't know about field hockey on the walk home. I wish I had her memory!

Winn is really keen to come to my next game. Oh, and she loved the uniforms – just like I told you!

Gotta go. Winn and I are making everyone supper tonight. It's Kraft Dinner. My favorite!
Gene

PS
What's your favorite food?

Winn Is Still Looking at Pictures

Winn's mom came over and talked to my mom for a long time today before she left for the hospital. She and Winn also brought all of Winn's photos over in a box to the doghouse.

So, I'm lying here right now, and it's about midnight and Winn is still going through every single picture. I guess it helps her get to sleep. I remember when we went to the beach, and Winn and her mom looked at all the pictures.

Oh well, I'm going to sleep.
Gene

Nov. 15th

Winn's Going To Hate Me

Dear Toni,

Winn's diary was just sitting open beside her box of pictures and I thought it was probably okay to look at the pictures, but then I kind of ended up reading her diary. Then Winn started to wake up and I panicked and dropped the diary. Lucky for me, Winn is one of those people who wake up very slowly because when I was trying to pick up the diary, I dumped her pictures. They went everywhere. I think I got most of them, but there were hundreds all over the floor. I found one of me. And there was another picture of The Fly. On the bottom Winn had written "Drew, a really nice boy whose sister is sometimes mean and calls him The Fly." Maybe Winn's right, maybe it isn't very nice to call him that. After all, he did, in a way, risk his life by sticking up for me with Julia and her gang.

On the bottom of the picture of me Winn had written "My best friend." Would a best friend look through your stuff and then lie about it? Because that's what I did when Winn woke up and asked me what I was doing with her box of pictures and diary.

I wouldn't blame you if you decided not to be my friend.
Gene

Nov. 16th

Dear Toni,
Well, the day went great. Winn can get Sally to do just about anything. I wish Sally would do that for me.

I wanted to tell Winn all day about the diary and pictures, but I haven't yet, and it's probably too late because she has already started looking through them all. I think I'll just pull the blankets over my head and pretend I'm sleeping.

Gene

Nov. 17th

I Didn't *Really* Read Her Diary

Dear Toni,

I've been thinking that I don't really need to apologize to Winn about reading her diary because I didn't *really* read it. I had just started to read it when she woke up, so I didn't read hardly anything, and mostly it was just poems. I'm sure the picture thing is fine because Winn has shown me the pictures before. And, I've made a promise to never do it again.

Gene

You've Got a New Friend!

Winn has been bugging me about my journal. I have a very large note on it that says "Stay Out!!!" But Winn was curious, so I told her about the project. She wants to write to you also. I hope you don't mind Toni, but some day you're going to get a journal from Winn also. She said she'll start it after she fills up the diary she is writing in now. I'm sure she will ask you a bazillion questions. So, if for some reason in the future you meet Winn, you don't need to tell her about the diary thing. Okay? Please don't.

Nov. 18th

It's a Family Day!

Dear Toni,

Mom and Dad took Winn, Drew, and me to the pool today. It's the first day off Dad has had since we moved in. Mom said it was about time, and that people would just have to get their cars fixed in the morning or wait until tomorrow.

Winn wanted a picture of our family at the pool, so the woman at the front desk took a picture of all of us. Winn looked at it for a long time before she put it in her purse.

I hope that in forty years they find a way to keep pools clean without chlorine. My eyes are killing me.

Gene

PS
Winn went home today.

Nov. 20th

Big Field-Hockey Game!!!!

Dear Toni,
We have a big field-hockey game tomorrow. The Blewett Bulldogs are the second-best team in our league. Mom, Dad, Winn, and Drew are all coming to cheer me on!

I hope that I score a bunch of goals and we win!

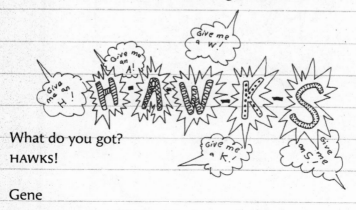

What do you got?
HAWKS!

Gene

Nov. 21st

No Goal but Three Assists

Dear Toni,

I got three assists! Drew had the whole crowd doing cheers for our team. Winn will probably tell you the names and numbers of everyone on my team; she memorized them all. Mom and Dad were jumping up and down and I felt like everything was just perfect. Winn got some great pictures of me playing. It was so cool! Oh yeah, and we WON!!!!!!!! First time in three years that our school has beat Blewett!

Time for bed.
Gene

PS
An assist feels almost as good as a goal, maybe even better!

Nov. 22nd

Great Day at School

Dear Toni,

    Tracy, our team captain, came up to me in the hall today and told me to thank Drew for helping us beat the Bulldogs. Even my coach said Drew was an all-star cheerleader! They both said to make sure I invited him to our next game. Tracy said that we should ask The Fly to be our team mascot. I didn't really answer because inside I was ready to burst – imagine; a fly for our team mascot!!!!! But then I thought about that whole thing with Julia and the picture Winn had written on and it didn't seem so funny anymore. So I told Tracy that I didn't call him The Fly anymore, because he's actually a pretty good brother. I wonder; do you have a brother?

Bye for now!
Gene

Nov. 23rd

Winn's Mom Is Sick. Really Sick!

Dear Toni,

Winn's mom needs to go back into the hospital, and now it looks like she'll be home for a few days, and then she is going to be away for a week or more. I asked Mom if Winn could just stay with us, but Mom said that under the circumstances it might be better for Winn to be with family. Winn's Uncle Jim from Saskatoon, Saskatchewan is flying up to stay with Winn and Kathy in the bus. He'll be here tomorrow.

Today is the first time that Winn has hardly said anything at all. Sally just laid her head on Winn's lap and let Winn pet her. Sally really understands Winn.

I can tell that Winn is scared about her mom. I'm scared about her mom too. What if she dies? If there is a heaven and you are there, Toni, could you please ask God to make sure that Winn's mom is going to be okay? I'd really appreciate that.

I wish no one ever died.
Gene

Nov. 24th

Another Call from Mr. Mackenzie!@#$**

Dear Toni,

Just what every kid needs. A teacher who calls home! That's right. Mr. Mackenzie called my parents, and now there is a meeting at school and we are going to discuss my goals and how I am not meeting them, or completing my schoolwork.

Mom is going to go berserk on me.

Gene

Nov. 25th

Winn's Uncle Is Here

Dear Toni,

Dad took Winn and me to the airport to pick up Winn's Uncle Jim. He works in the hospital in Saskatoon, and he's really nice. Jim is the uncle that bought Winn the Polaroid camera.

Dad told Jim that he'd lend him our rust bucket and when I started to apologize to Jim about the different-colored door and fender, he said he didn't care about that at all. He said he was just grateful that his sister and niece had such wonderful neighbors and friends. Dad rubbed his glove into my hair and smiled. I guess the old car is good for something after all.

Goodnight, Toni. I hope everything in your life is great.
Gene

Nov. 27th

A Date with Winn and Her Uncle Jim

Dear Toni,

Winn and her Uncle Jim are going to spend most of their time at the hospital and the library today. Winn asked if it would be okay if she and her uncle picked me up from school, so that I could go bowling and to the Burger Barn. Winn's uncle invited Drew too.

I know that Winn was asking about picking me up from school because of what happened with Julia last time. But I told her that it was fine ANYTIME! It really is, too.

I told her that Drew and I would wait outside on the bench for her, and if she wanted to see my class, I'd

take her in and show her and her Uncle Jim my desk
and stuff. Winn's never even been in a school; she's
always been homeschooled.

Gene

Nov. 28th

The Dreaded Meeting

Dear Toni,

    I sure hope you never have to sit outside your class
before school starts and wait for a meeting to begin
with your parents and your teacher. There we were,
three silent statues, waiting for the dreaded meeting to
begin. Mom kept on taking deep breaths and Dad just
read the paper.

    The whole time I was trying to come up with a
really good excuse for not meeting any of the science
project deadlines. But the truth is, when I leave school
these days I just sort of forget about everything until
the next day when the bell rings. And the part about
me not meeting my goals, I have. But how was I
suppose to tell everyone that I lied about the goals
I taped to my desk?

The meeting was just as awful as I thought. Mom thought I'd been doing my homework, because as she put it, every time she asked me to do anything, I'd say I was working on my project. Then Mr. Mackenzie told Mom and Dad that he was pretty sure that the journal project and the dogs had gotten in the way of my homework.

In the end *everybody* – and that did NOT include me – decided that I needed to leave my journal until I make an effort to catch up on my homework and class work! Then my parents said if that didn't help, they would get Drew to take care of the dogs. I told them that was capital punishment, and it's illegal for kids. Mom says she knows how much I like writing to you, so she and I are going to work twenty minutes every day after school, until I'm caught up.

I'm being held hostage AGAIN!
Gene

Nov. 29th

Winn Has To Go to Saskatchewan

Dear Toni,

Mom says that I can write to you because of the bad news. Winn's Uncle Jim and the doctors have agreed that it's best if Kathy is transferred to a hospital in Saskatoon, so she'll be closer to her family. She can get treatments there and her parents can take of Winn. Winn's going to be leaving on Sunday night. She has to fly by herself to Saskatoon and her grandparents will pick her up at the airport. Kathy and Jim are going to fly when all the arrangements are made.

Mom went through all our boxes of winter stuff. Drew has grown out of his parka and snow pants, and Winn's feet are smaller than mine, so we decided that we should send the things we've outgrown with her.

Just hauling all that stuff out of the garage and into the shoebox made me want winter. Winn has always lived in Mexico during the winter and she has never ever seen real snow. It was fun to see all my old things, but it made me homesick. I told Winn how snow can be as light as dust, or very wet and heavy, and about how no two snowflakes are alike. Winn says she thinks that snowflakes must be a lot like people, because she has never met two who were the same. I showed her how to make a snow angel. Winn says that if there's lots of snow when she gets to Saskatchewan, she'll go outside, lie down in the snow, and make a snow angel for me, Sally, the pups, Drew, and one for her mom.

Drew gave her the best advice. "NEVER, EVER touch your tongue to frozen monkey bars, because you'll have to rip the first hundred thousand layers of skin off to get it unstuck." And believe me, he knows!

Then Winn and I went out to the doghouse. I know that it's just something about Winn that she won't look at me when I talk to her, but I decided to ask her why she doesn't. Winn just kept looking into her hands, and then she said that she *does* like to look at people's faces, just not in their eyes too much. But always, when she starts looking at their faces, they become so interesting that she keeps looking and looking and looking. Then people get mad and tell her it's rude. So she just doesn't look because it always gets her into trouble. Winn says that pictures don't yell. I promised not to yell, and told Winn she could look at me. When Winn lifted her face I couldn't believe it, but you know, I've never really looked at her, either. I didn't know her eyes were so brown or that she had so many little freckles on the edges of her cheeks. Not as many as me, but then not many people do. Winn didn't exactly look at my eyes, but I could tell that she was really looking at my face. At first I almost cried, and then I just said it as quick as I could. "I'm sorry about snooping in your pictures and the diary thing." Winn looked at me and lifted up her eyebrows really high and said, "I know." I don't know why, but we both started laughing and I almost peed my pants.

Drew came in and started making the weirdest faces and pulling down his eyelids. He can even bug out his eyes. Then he really looks like a fly. We all laughed until we hurt. Sally and the pups just sat there, staring at us.

Winn looked at Sally and asked her if she thought we were all crazy. But we all knew what Sally was thinking, and when Winn looked at me, I had to say it. "Sally wants you to give her a hug." Sally's tail began to thump against the floor and the moment Winn opened her mouth to ask her, Sally *woofed* and made a gigantic leap almost into Winn's lap. Sally tucked her nose up under Winn's chin, and Winn wrapped her arms around her. The two of them sat there for a long time and it made me happy.

Gene

PS

I wonder if Sally understands when I tell her Winn's leaving, and that maybe she's leaving forever.

Nov. 30th

Last Day

Dear Toni,
    Today was hard. Winn didn't want to do anything,
so we just hung out with the dogs and looked through
all of her pictures. Sally followed Winn everywhere.
    It's different being the person who isn't moving.
I'm kind of mad at Kathy for getting sick and ruining
everything. I know it's stupid to think that way. It's just
that, in a way, she ruined everything.

I'll talk to you tomorrow.
Gene

Dec. 1st

Good-Bye, Winn

Dear Toni,
    Winn left today. She said that when she does her
journal she'll write for a hundred days, just like I have
done, and send it to the museum when it's full. I'm
sure she will because she is a very organized person.

Maybe she'll be back living here, and we can take it there together.

Anyway, I hate saying good-bye.
Gene

Dec. 2nd

Winn Is in Saskatchewan

Dear Toni,
    Winn's Uncle Jim came over to the doghouse this morning before school and told me that Winn is at the farm and there's snow. Lots of it!
    He said that Winn made one hundred and thirty-two snow angels in a circle all around her grandparents' house! He brought over a box of treats for Sally, and Winn's guitar and beginner chord book for me. He said that Winn wanted me to have it.

I wish I could send Winn something.
Gene

Dec. 6th

Kathy and Jim Are Gone

Dear Toni,

   I know it's been days since I wrote to you, but I just didn't have anything to say and I haven't caught up on my homework. I know that I'm not supposed to write in my journal until I've finished it all, but I just feel like I need to talk to someone, and it's been four days since I've written to you.

   Kathy and Jim left, and the bus is sitting over there empty. No gray smoke is floating up from the little chimney at the back. The curtains are pulled tight and I miss hearing Winn's mom play her guitar at night. Sally still stands up every time someone comes to the doghouse door, and I can tell that she's really disappointed when it's not Winn.

   It'll be Christmas soon. Winn and I had some great ideas for decorating the doghouse. I wish you could tell me the future, Toni. I wish you could tell me if Winn and her mom will be back.

From all of us at the lonely doghouse,
Gene

Dec. 7th

The Lees Are Coming Back

Dear Toni,

Dad says that the gas station owners are going to be back from Mexico some time before Christmas, and that I need to keep my head about the dogs. He and Mom said that they know how much I love Sally and her puppies and promise that I can have a dog when we get a place of our own. Mom said that if the Lees sell the pups, I can buy one of them. But I could never take one of Sally's pups away from her. Never.

Why do all good things have to come to an end?
Gene

Dec. 8th

Winn Is Gone for Good

Dear Toni,

Winn's uncle called and he told me that Winn had a hundred questions for me about Sally and the pups and that she misses me.

The worst thing is that Winn is going to stay at her grandparents' farm. A friend of theirs is planning to come and pick up the bus. Dad told Jim that he'll get it running smoothly for them.

Bye for now,
Gene

Inside the Bus

I'm just sitting here at the tiny little kitchen table in the bus, while Dad works on the engine. I drew a picture of me with Sally and the pups, and Mom and I put it in a frame that says "Best Friends." I made a card that says "We all miss Winn!" I'm going to leave it on her shelf beside the bed.

Gene

Dec. 9th

My Grandparents Are Coming

Dear Toni,
     My grandma and grandpa are coming this weekend. Drew and I get to stay at the hotel with them both nights. Mom has offered to watch the dogs while we're at the hotel.

Gotta go.
Gene

Dec. 10th

That Was F-U-N!!!!!

Dear Toni,
     It's great to have a grandma and a grandpa. We ate at the restaurant and swam in the pool. I thought about Winn with her grandma and grandpa on the farm. I hope they are as nice as my grandparents. Grandma took Drew and me out shopping for new school clothes and professional haircuts! No more missing bangs!

Gene

PS
Do you like my new haircut?

...my new haircut...

↑ very
even edges

Dec. 12th

We're Saving a Whack of Money!

Dear Toni,

Mom and Dad are talking about buying a new
trailer and putting it in the Silver Star Trailer Park. I
guess we are saving a whack of money!

In a way I'm real excited about the new trailer, but
I'm not excited about leaving Sally and the pups. It's

only been six weeks, but I feel like I have spent my whole life with them and I don't want it to end.

Your pen pal who is more dog than human,
Gene

Dec. 13th

New Kid at School

Dear Toni,

There's a new girl in our class and her name is Anne. She seems really nice. Anne really likes dogs, and her family has a Jack Russell named Rosie. She invited me over tomorrow after school. Anne says that Rosie is real smart, but kind of feisty.

The best thing is that she and her family live in the Silver Star. Maybe one day we'll be neighbors.

Gene

Dec. 14th

The Bus Is Gone

Dear Toni,
  When I came home from school today the bus was gone. Dad says that as long as you remember someone, they never really leave you. I'm not so sure about that because I remember Winn really well, but it doesn't feel like she's here anymore. It just feels like she's gone, forever.
  Mom told me that we'll try to visit Winn and her mom. She said she wasn't making any promises about when, only that she'd get me there somehow. I guess I always hoped that as long as the bus was here, Winn might come back. But I don't think so anymore.

Gene

Dec. 15th

I Feel Sick

Dear Toni,
  I'm home today. Mostly, I just don't feel like doing anything. I don't even feel like playing with the pups.

Every time I go into the doghouse, I start thinking about Winn and how I didn't like her in the beginning and how she's now the best friend I have, and she's gone.

Sometimes I wonder if Winn's mom is going to die. If I could have one wish, it would be for Kathy to get better. Nothing else. But I'm not even sure I still believe in wishes. I've had lots of wishes that never came true. People always say not to tell anyone if you want a wish to come true. I never told anyone lots of my wishes and most of them never came true. Maybe it's stupid to wish for anything, especially something as important as someone not dying.

Gene

Dec. 16th

Chocolate-Chip Cookies

Dear Toni,

Anne called and invited me over. I didn't want to go, but in the end it was fun. Her mom let us make a gigantic batch of chocolate-chip oatmeal cookies. Anne is going to bring them to school. She says that even though we made them at her house, they're from both of us, and I can help her hand them out.

I told Anne all about Winn and how she was a really good photographer and really good with the dogs. Anne says she can't imagine Sally liking anyone more than she likes me.

Rosie sure is a feisty little dog. Anne and I played her favorite game. Rosie runs around and around in circles, and we have to try and get her raggy dog toy from her. We laughed a ton!

Your full-of-cookie-dough pen pal,
Gene

PS
I would have saved you a cookie, but I don't think it would keep for forty years. Just so you know, they were great!!!!!

PPS
I drew Sally next to Rosie to show you the difference in their sizes. They don't know each other yet. I think that Rosie might be a little too nasty around the pups for Sally.

Dec. 17th

The Lees Are On Their Way

Dear Toni,

    Mr. and Mrs. Lee called and they'll be here Wednesday. We don't have to move or anything. The Lees have a big house near the river. Mr. Lee told Dad that two of the three pups are already spoken for. I didn't know that. I wonder who is left. I also wonder how it will be for Sally to lose her pups.

    Dad says it's different for dogs than it is for people. I don't think so. I think people don't really understand dogs very well. Drew agrees with me.

    Dad says I should think about asking Mr. Lee if I can buy the one pup that is left. A part of me wants to, but I don't want to take Sally's last puppy when the other two are already gone.

Maybe if I don't buy the last pup, Mr. Lee will keep it and Sally together.

Gene

Dec. 18th

A Card From Winn

Dear Toni,

Winn sent Drew and me each one of her pictures made into a card. Mine is of her in all the snow clothes standing beside her grandparents' barn. Winn says that she loves snow and has made a bazillion (Winn used to say that there was no such word as *bazillion*; I guess she's changed her mind) snow angels.

Soon I'll be finished caring for the dogs. And soon I'll be finished this writing project. We only have this week left before they go to the museum. It's so amazing to think about you reading my journal in forty years. I think that you and I would have been really good friends. Don't you?

Gene

Dec. 20th

The Lees Are Home

Dear Toni,

    The Lees got home today, and Mr. Lee came right over to see the dogs. He gave me a hundred and fifty dollars for taking care of them while they were away. He and I sat in the doghouse for a long time, and he looked through my project notes on the pups. He said that if he were the teacher, he'd give me an A+, and he could tell by the notes, drawings, and photographs that the dogs had been well cared for while he and Mrs. Lee were away. I told him that Winn took most of the pictures and that Sally mostly cared for the pups.

    I told him how Sally was such a great mother, and how much she had liked Winn. He said he knew that Sally was a great mother because she'd had several litters before. I asked him if Sally had been real sad when her other pups left. He said that she had been, but caring for pups was a pretty demanding job for her. He thinks that when these puppies are finally ready to go to good homes, Sally will be fed up with all their fooling around. "After all," he said, "she's going to be seven years old next spring." That means that she's about forty-nine in human years. Which is almost as old as I'll be when you read this. I'll be ancient!

I'm not sure what I'm going to do with the money. I think I'll save it and go to see Winn.

But for now, I'm RICH!
Gene

The Favor

Mr. Lee came by again today. He thanked me over and over for doing such a good job with the dogs. So I guess I did okay. Later, he came out to the doghouse with Dad and asked if I could do him a big favor. He and Mrs. Lee have decided to spend more time in the sun. Mr. Lee said he knew that I might want a puppy, but that if I hadn't made my mind up yet, he would like me to consider taking Sally.

He told me I could have Boxer if that was what I really wanted and he'd understand. He also said he was sure he could find a good home for Sally if I didn't want her. I could hardly keep from blurting out YES! from the moment I knew he was telling me that Sally was mine. Isn't that amazing Toni? Sally is mine!!!!

Mr. Lee gave me Sally's doghouse. Then he said I could also have her harness. "What harness?" I asked. He showed me the leather harness they used when they took Sally for a walk. I guess Winn was right about that. Mr. Lee said we were lucky she didn't pull us all the way to the river. I get to have both the doghouse and the harness for free, and Mom and Dad were totally fine with the idea! I can't believe it. Sally is mine! I wonder if they'll let me buy Boxer.

Your very happy friend,
Gene

Dec. 21st

Time Is Running Out

Dear Toni,
Just one more day until our journals go to the museum. It's going to be strange not writing to you. I asked if I could give the museum curator a note to tell you about everything that happens with the trailer and moving and that maybe she'd put it in with my journal. Mr. Mackenzie said he'd think about it, but in the end he said no, because the journals were all going

to be sealed in a time capsule. The whole idea behind
a time capsule is that it stays closed until the date
you have chosen to open it. I guess my life will
probably be full of things that I would have wanted to
share with you.

Your soon-not-to-be pen pal,
Gene

A Call from Winn's Uncle

Winn's Uncle Jim called to tell us that Winn and
Kathy's bus arrived, safe and sound. While I was telling
Winn's Uncle Jim about me getting Sally, a fantastic
idea popped into my head. Sally always loved Winn
more than me. So I asked Mom and Dad if it was okay
to spend some of my money to buy Boxer, and give
Sally to Winn. Jim said if I was sure that was what I
wanted to do, he'd pay the freight for us to fly Sally
to Saskatoon.

I called Mr. Lee to tell him about my idea, and let
him know that I wanted Boxer. Mr. Lee said that Boxer
is mine. Mine for FREE!!!! He loved the idea of giving
Sally to Winn. He said it's perfect, because Sally was
born on a farm and she'd love it in Saskatchewan.

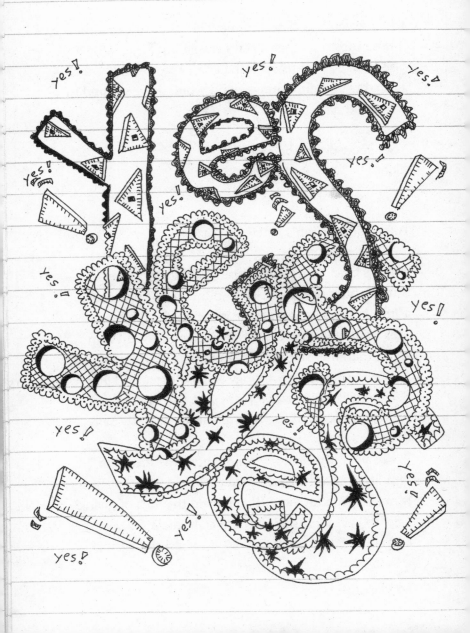

So here is the big news of the day: *SALLY, SUPREME ST. BERNARD WILL BE MOVING TO SASKATOON, SASKATCHEWAN!!!!* Well, actually to a farm outside of Saskatoon, but Saskatoon is where the airport is.

I can't wait to tell Sally; this will be the best surprise ever, and Winn will be so happy!
Gene

PS
Nothing new has happened with finding a trailer. Anne and I are hoping that the two empty lots don't fill up before my parents find the right trailer to buy.

Why do adults always take so long to make up their minds about good things when they are so quick to decide about things they don't want?

One of the lots is only three down from Anne and it's big enough for the doghouse. Mom says she and Dad are moving as fast as they can, but that this is much more important than deciding what to put on your popcorn at the movies. I guess so. But I wish they'd hurry up!

Your pen pal, who is always waiting forever,
Gene

A Gift from Sally

Mr. Lee brought over a gigantic crate for us to ship
Sally to Saskatoon. I get to go with him and Dad to
the airport. Mr. Lee says that the pups are ready to be
without their mother. Winn's uncle is going to pick
Sally up and take her out to the farm.

I hope the puppies are not too lonely. It will be
really sad to say good-bye to Sally, but I know she will
be very, very happy to be with Winn. The pups get to
hang out in the *shoebox* until their new families pick
them up. I hope they understand that Sally is going to
be with Winn. I know Sally understands, because when
I told her, she looked at me and tilted her head and
really listened. Then I thought I'd try one more time
and I asked her for a hug. You won't believe it, but she
wagged her whole body over to me and tucked her
nose up under my chin and leaned into me – just like
she used to with Winn. I wrapped my arms around
her the way Winn did, and I promised Sally that Shady
and Lucy were going to good homes and I'd take care
of Boxer for his whole life. And that is a promise I
promise to keep. Forever!

Gene

Dec. 22nd

The Last Journal Entry

Dear Toni,

This morning we are all sitting at our desks writing our last journal entry and it is snowing the largest flakes I have ever seen. Boxer is spending his first day with my dad. Shady and Lucy were picked up this morning. Sally was pretty groggy from the medication the vet gave her when she got into her crate at the airport last night. She'll probably be that way until Winn's Uncle Jim picks her up. Sally is my Christmas present to Winn. I think it's the best Christmas gift I have ever given anyone. And I guess that maybe this journal is my Christmas gift to you. I hope you like it.

I hate good-byes. It feels like my whole life is about saying good-bye to everyone. Even though you weren't ever REALLY here, you were real to me. Maybe your name isn't even Toni, but you've been Toni to me, and I am going to miss you a lot. I hope my life wasn't too boring.

Drew says good-bye, so do Mom and Dad, and so does Anne. She wishes she had come in time to do her own journal. Maybe in forty years you'll write back to me and I'll get to meet you. That would be GREAT!

I hope you like the bookmark. It's a picture of Boxer and me. It's been a lot of fun writing to you.

Your friend forever from forty years ago,
Gene Tucks

Dec. 22nd

Forty Years Later

Dear Gene,

Today we went on a field trip to Maple Grove Park. When we got there, the museum curator brought out the time capsule with all of the journals from your 6th-Grade class. She told us that you planted the maple trees for us when you were in Grade 6, and about the history of Maple Grove. Your school was torn down about ten years ago. I'm glad they left the trees. They are beautiful and gigantic! I play soccer in Maple Grove Park all summer.

We all sat under the maple trees, read our journals, and ate lunch. I moved to the eleventh tree after I read that you planted it for me. Your life was definitely not boring! I really liked the way you started out by calling me Nobody and then Somebody and then Toni. I also really like how you called your brother The Fly. But I agree that a brother who sticks up for you when you need him, is a brother who should not be called The Fly.

The curator asked if I would donate your original journal to the museum collection. She's going to make a copy of it for me. Yours was the thickest journal from your class, and you were the only person who had put doodle drawings in their journal. The curator also wanted to keep it together with Winn's journal and Polaroid photo collection. Her journal wasn't in the time capsule, but the curator said that I could come to the museum and see it any time. She said that there are loads of photographs of you and Sally and Winn. I can't wait to see what you really looked like. I hope that Winn's mom didn't die. I also think it was great that you gave Sally to Winn. Even though it isn't Christmas for a few days, I think this will be my favorite present.

Our class is going to try and find all the people from your Grade-6 class and send you each a copy of your journal. I hope I find you. Then we are going to start our own journal project. I want to write to you, because I know that you would be really glad that someone actually got your journal — and loved it.

Your friend from the future,
Toni

PS
Your doodles are fantabulous! (I like to make up new words.) And I think the bookmark you made me is grandific! My teacher wants me to give it to the museum and keep a copy, but the curator said it's up to me.

What do you think I should do?

About the Author

My favorite way to begin the day is to wake up early, make a pot of tea, and watch the sunrise from my front porch. But like other people, I eventually need to go to work. For the past twenty years, I have worked with kids of all ages as a storyteller, sign language interpreter, children's library assistant, math and ESL tutor, and, most recently, teacher's assistant. I love art, music, and learning new things, but more than anything, I love to laugh with my family and friends.